הלב הוא
קטמנדו

the heart

is

Katmandu

ALSO BY YOEL HOFFMANN
Available from New Directions

Bernhard

The Christ of Fish

Katschen & The Book of Joseph

the heart
is
katmandu

YOEL
HOFFMANN

Translated from the Hebrew
by Peter Cole

NEW DIRECTIONS

The Heart Is Katmandu is published by arrangement with the
Harris/Elon Agency and the Keter Publishing Company of
Israel.

Design by Semadar Megged
First published clothbound in 2001
Manufactured in the United States of America.
New Directions Books are printed on acid-free paper.
Published simultaneously in Canada by Penguin Books
Canada Limited.

Library of Congress Cataloging-in-Publication Data:

Hoffmann, Yoel.
[Lev hu Katmandu. English]
The heart is Katmandu / Yoel Hoffmann ; translated by Peter
Cole.
p. cm.
ISBN 0-8112-1465-6 (alk. paper)
I. Cole, Peter, 1957–   II. Title.
PJ5054.H6319L4813   2001
892.4'36—dc21   00-069567

New Directions Books are published for James Laughlin
by New Directions Publishing Corporation
80 Eighth Avenue, New York 10011

הלב הוא
קטמנדו

the heart
is
katmandu

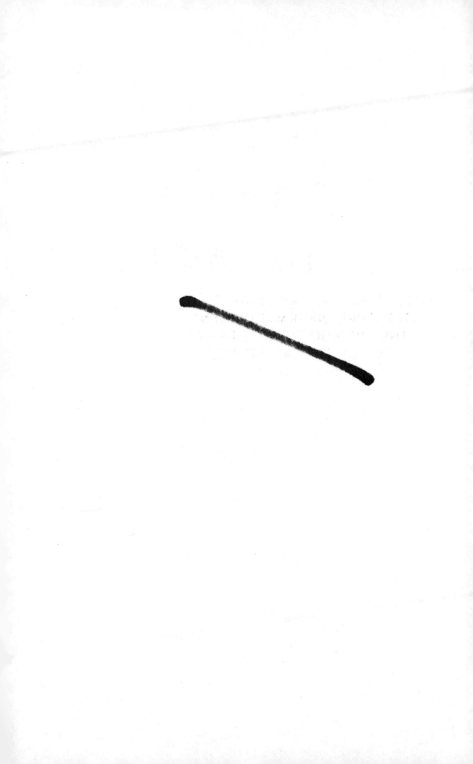

BOOK ONE

1

AT AGE 43, Yehoahim seldom ate cucumbers. Sights distracted him (how Ehud Vazana washes his Ford Fiesta under the poplar tree while small birds chirp over his head, et cetera).

People come and say things to him like *Erlakan. Erlakan?* He thinks: Why, that's the name of the primary substance. He lifts his blue-gray eyes (like the eyes of Prince What's-his-name in *War and Peace*) to the sky.

2

Yesterday, for instance, he ran into Batya.

Behind her he saw the coast of Acre and the refineries and, nevertheless, he asked in an ordinary manner: "How are you?"

How *are you?!* (he thought later). For how might she be? The five toes of each foot (hers and mine), and together that makes twenty. . . .

Incredibly, a large mastiff crosses the street, and this (Yehoahim thinks) is the right side whereas Lilith* (who was re- born as Batya) is the left and the measure of judgment, which is devoid of mercy, al- though she said "Fine," and said "thank you."

3

Batya walks up Moriah Street, whereas Yehoahim buys a paper (*HaAretz*) and casts a spell on the Discount Bank.

At the corner of Ocean Boulevard, he or- ders an espresso with milk, and from where he sits (from the edge of his head) a chimney opens out and his thoughts run through it like the Orient Express.

---

*Lilith—Adam's wife before Eve: a seducer of men, from whose nocturnal emissions she bears an infinite number of demonic sons.

4

It is extremely important to know *what* Yehoahim is thinking.

The mantle of the world is double. It encircles the outermost stars, and when it returns it encircles the skulls.

Sometimes (when the stars are pale before the day) the flesh is transparent. Then one can see how the organs within lean toward each other over and over. And when a person says something (Oy, for example), enormous flames of fire on the sun answer him.

It's four in the afternoon, and now the mastiff is standing where Rose of the Carmel Street begins.

Time inches along. One minute pushes up against the next, as in the workers' strike by the factory gate.

5

German immigrants pass by the café, and also the large letter *tzaddik*.*

And because it is late afternoon, the trees' shadows are longer now. But what (Yehoahim thinks) is a shadow.

A shadow (he thinks) is like a thought. The upside-down reflection of something larger.

I (he thinks) am the shadow's shadow. And therefore he no longer cares, and says, "Hey, Itzik."

6

Itzik holds out one of his hands (the other he keeps in reserve) and says "What's up?"

The mastiff's back is lit with a reddish glow. Cranes fly south (to warmer climes) and some of the angels over Itzik's head (his gabardine pants are held in place by a

* *The eighteenth letter of the Hebrew alphabet*

yellow belt made of suede) fly off a short
distance and return, like children whose
mother is calling them home for dinner.

7

Itzik says: "Yesterday I ran into Shula"
(though actually he says: These two hands
I'm waving might be three).

　Yehoahim says: "Didn't she get married?" (And actually he says: If the sea
rose up to the edge of the mountain and
everything.)

Variatzia the waitress comes and goes during this conversation, her heels clicking
against the floor (*Derabbanan* . . . *derabbanan* . . .).*

A great wind rises up from the wadis and
whistles through the end-of-the-season
sales.

---

* *"Of our rabbis"* (*Aramaic*), *as in* Kaddish Derabbanan—*the
rabbis' kaddish.*

8

What is suffering for? (Yehoahim thinks).

Take a roof. Take a mountain. Take a tree.

What? What?

9

Should I assemble myself (he thinks) out of memories?

For I wasn't like that, and like that, and like that. Someone, after all, named me Yehoahim, and then said to himself: "This is Yehoahim."

Where is my father—whose name, Ephraim, I barely remember?

In some strange way he watched them moving his bed toward the last window.

10

It turns out that birds do in fact say "chirp," Yehoahim thinks.

He tells himself the story of the dead woman: There was a woman who was born very late. Seventy years, perhaps, after she came into the world. People asked her: Where have you been all this time, et cetera.

Meanwhile, the colors of the sky are shifting, and on the table Itzik unfolds a lease.

11

In the small room, he says, you'll be able to have guests over.

The hoopoe, Yehoahim thinks.

The lease is written out, line after line, and in all sorts of places Yehoahim needs to set down his initials.

He writes YH YH YH and between the Y and the H he places a period.

The mastiff is now standing on the other side of the street (in the world, if you like).

12

Hallelujah!

The sun finally sets and, as though at a concert, an invisible director turns on the street lights.

Variatzia the waitress gathers the coffee cups and wipes off the table with a damp cloth.

Maybe because of the cloth, or the motion of her hand, or her fingernails, which are red, Yehoahim is suddenly filled with joy.

13

At night, strange figures come to Yehoahim:

There's a lion, and though behind it one can see the sea, one cannot call it a sea lion.

A cook, or a woman cook. The woman who warmed his first milk.

A toy rhinoceros.

If he turned over in his sleep, he did so weightlessly, with the motion of a book

lying open in a field as a gust of wind
comes across it.

14

The first foot that Yehoahim puts down
onto the floor is the foot of morning (from
which the sight of the window is formed,
along with the sun behind it).

Edith Piaf sings *je ne regrette rien*. Yehoahim takes an umbrella out of the closet
and walks from corner to corner like the
chapters in a history book (Napoleon's
conquests, et cetera).

15

In the kitchen there stands a clay pot, and
in it—a philodendron.
   No one knows its first name, but it has a
discernable shape—a leaf . . . a leaf
. . . a leaf . . . a leaf. It continues today
what was started yesterday.

O the sun (Yehoahim thinks), *le soleil*.
The dermatologist.

16

Suddenly, for no reason, his heart breaks.

His red heart which has seen all sorts of things—streets, candles burning in the night, countless feet—this heart gives way out of loneliness and fear.

There is no longer anything to hold on to (Yehoahim thinks) and he weeps like a jackal, or an owl, or a legendary river that sweeps along what it sweeps along, with neither purpose nor end.

17

Now he is thinking:
    I had a dog and the dog died.
    I had a woman and she went away.

I have seen cadavers. The empty shell of a man, and I have heard the terrible sound lying beneath the world.

He lies in bed and counts his limbs: Ten.
Two. One. In a little while (he thinks) his
heart will go still.

18

The sun in the window begins to rise
and at roughly seven-thirty morning descends.

The voices whisper to him: Open the
umbrella! Open the umbrella! But his
hands are frozen with fear.

He sees an old house he lived in once.
Stairs he climbed. The old dog comes
toward him. A woman sits at the table.
But *he* goes up backwards.

19

Now he is breathing. From his open
mouth there rise the two giraffes whose
necks are glowing with a phosphorescent
light, and there rises the wild boar, and
the antelope, whose name alone makes it
leap, and the reed-birds whose turquoise
color is only—for an instant—now and

then revealed, and the *leerot*, which are made of the stuff of dreams and whose bodies crumble before the light, as well as the swift water-mice, and extremely dark, limbless creatures composed of the bodies of memories.

20

Like the water cow that lowers its head and sees, for a moment, the murky green, he asks himself:

What *else* do I have to do? Inquire about something in a shop? Write to a certain office?

His thighbone is weak, and his left foot will go (he knows) somewhere else. Chinese ladies holding delicate fans waft a breeze over their faces and, with gentle voices, ask the foot: Wong Way?

The ears are directed toward the large grasshoppers, standing there motionless, and the right hand (a sign, as it were, of life) agrees to die because what . . .

Suddenly he's thinking about soccer fans ("jerks . . .").

21

Now birds are chirping because morning is poised, nevertheless, outside with its myriad names (like *Morgen,* or *asa*).*

What good (Yehoahim thinks) is sorrow. After all, one can see that everything is transparent, and it's doubtful that "transparent" is a word, because it itself is transparent (or because it's a thing like all other things that might fall or be bent or get lost).

If he wasn't embarrassed he'd step (like the children) between the floor tiles, for what has he got to lose?

Morning (German and Japanese)

22

The sun (he thinks) is somewhat blue.

The kitchen utensils are arrayed like cattle on a hot day and it's forbidden to say anything psychological about them, that the pot, for example, represses its feelings.

Especially the forks (he thinks). One rinses them off, and water drips from them, but their prongs point upward like Beethoven's four chords.

23

Why (he thinks) break the egg?

Happiness will rise without effort from suffering, like marsh vapors.

Outside, a cock crows because its mother has gone away.

24

The plates are transparent, and it's possible to see the table through them, and if one passes through it, and then through

the floor toward the ground and onward,
one can see the innermost stars.

Whatever shines at depths such as
these (Yehoahim thinks) reaches the
chambers of the heart.

The cock crows for a second time because
its mother has gone to Katmandu, and he
is young, and every night the sun sinks
and he doesn't know if it will rise again.

25

Now, as he strips off his pajama bottoms,
it is impossible to be mistaken about
Yehoahim's legs. Leaves of ivy on the
other side of the window remind him of
the word "love."

In a little while it will be winter
(he thinks) and I am going to a new
house. . . .

(Suddenly the words lose their power
and it seems to him that they themselves
are going away.)

About other things he has no doubt. The
hundred-watt bulb, for instance, which

hangs at the exact middle of the room, and which he calls the "little sun," or the closet, which contains a kind of closet-air—he calls it "Nitza" (and the closet answers him: "What?").

26

And there's also the cockroach that sometimes, on its way from one place to another, on its six legs, passes beneath the little sun.

About the cockroach Yehoahim has the following thoughts:

a) "Here's the cockroach."
b) There is a God on high.
c) Mercy. That is, the mercy God extends to His creatures.
d) Distance. That is, what stands between him and the cockroach forever.
e) The cockroach's nothingness. That is, the cockroach seen in the light of truth.
f) His own nothingness, from within which the cockroach reemerges as in "a) 'Here's the cockroach'."

27

Hallelujah!

Though Yehoahim's mouth is full of toothpaste, the telephone rings because it's brimming with human signals.

Through the long cord comes Itzik's voice, and it is impossible to say what he's saying, because Yehoahim hears only the news of the voice's existence in the world, even though man is mysterious, and one needs to call out like a quail, or a widow, Where art thou?

28

It's extremely difficult to describe the conversation on account of the noise made by the heavenly bodies.

Planets grow distant from each other, and when Itzik says, When will you come, it's extremely difficult to know just *where* Yehoahim might come to.

What does not alter are the forms of thought: pants and all (when one thinks of pants) and therefore the person there and the person here (each of whom holds in his hand a receiver). . . . And woe unto us who have forgotten (for we, too, are in this world) the one thing that we knew. The thing whose color is somewhat blue.

29

A fine wind blows across Yehoahim's face, like women who say Thank God when they take off their shoes.

At the corner of Ocean Boulevard he orders an espresso with milk and waits for Itzik. As in a story pregnant with meaning, the mastiff again stands across the street, and behind him—between him and the travel agency—bougainvillea.

The waitress Variatzia once again clicks (*derabbanan, derabbanan*) and the birds, too, again confirm the sound that has long been a fixture in the cultures of man.

30

Someone (Yehoahim thinks) stretched taut that blue sheet and scattered stains of cloud across it. These are the upper waters, and the lower waters (he thinks) are the cucumber.

When Itzik arrives, Yehoahim sees that a kind of halo accompanies him. The bottom of his pants flap about in the air, and it is impossible to know if it's the air that's in motion or the pants.

31

Itzik puts a ring of keys on the table and says: Yesterday I saw Shula.

Yehoahim is thinking: Wasn't I here before? Haven't I heard these things? But he asks: Didn't she get married?

Suddenly he sees Itzik's suffering behind his face. There is no other suffering (he thinks) like this in the world. A light green, somewhat cool.

32

Now Itzik is talking about Shula, and it's clear that he carefully washes his clothes. Shula (Yehoahim thinks) is already implicated in the stuff of the world and, in just a short while, will emerge from the entrance to her house in Romema or Neveh Sha'anan like a marten.

Itzik selects a yellow key on the ring and holds it up as one raises a conductor's baton. This, he says, is to the front door.

33

At the front door (Yehoahim thinks) the talking jackal will stand.

Like Saint Peter at the Pearly Gates, the talking jackal will greet (with a howl) those who come.

Professor What's-his-name from the Technical Institute will come, and Irena the chemist.

Someone will serve them Viennese coffee, and they'll talk about this and that. But the talking jackal will not turn its head toward them, as his job is to guard the door. Only his tail will rise and fall.

At nine-thirty Edelstein the surgeon will come with his wife, Penina . . .

34

Suddenly the mastiff is standing right by the table behind Itzik's back.

Now, for the first time, Yehoahim can speak in a language that isn't foreign to him, and he draws the words from the place where they come into being. What is said is forgotten a moment before it's uttered, and even Itzik, Itzik the bird, Itzik the crane . . .

35

Women walk out of the supermarket, carrying all sorts of things in very thin bags.

Give me a woman (Yehoahim thinks) who will carry something for me and the dog. A drawer, or a jar of mustard, or a screwdriver, or a frying pan, or a porcelain horse, or a scroll, or a plum cake, or a baby, or the word "or" itself, even though

they no longer stretch nylon stockings
along their legs like they used to, when the
weave would unravel and they'd call that
place a run . . .

"What" Itzik asks suddenly, as though
from within the sun.

36

Who is writing (Yehoahim thinks) the
story of my life? A ghost writer?

A crow and the Ukraine get confused in
his thoughts. One might be the other and
the other the one (he thinks).

Meanwhile, he sees the street's reflection
in a glass of water. Whoever walks by
there, walks through the glass as well.

37

You need (he says to himself) to go
further.

Beyond these reflections there is pain, damn it, and how can I (he thinks) know which death gave birth to it?

The word death seems strange to him, but he knows that he should not dwell on it, for death itself lacks the letter "d" or "t" . . .

38

Opposite, at the hardware store, a man is taking ladders out to the street. Now the mastiff is walking down Ocean Boulevard.

"Shall we go there?" Itzik asks, and Yehoahim thinks: There? There? There? There?

(Toes, he thinks, are the foot's fingers.)

39

On the way to Margoliot Street, Itzik finds five shekels. Yehoahim recalls the name Avrushmi.

"From the window," Itzik says, "you can see the beach at Atlit."

By the door, Itzik singles out the yellow key on the key chain.

Oy, Yehoahim thinks, like Moses . . .

40

Now Itzik is looking for the key to the bedroom. Outside someone is calling: Svetlana . . .

Two years to the end of the second millennium and, miraculously, the sky isn't falling.

41

In the distance Yehoahim sees the beach at Atlit. Memories come back to him in fragments: for example, his father carrying him (as Joyce the father, drunk, carried James the child) toward the toy fair.

"You see?" Itzik says, "Didn't I tell you?"

42

At night, a great deal of water runs down from the high places and gathers in tiny streams in the street.

In a little while, Yehoahim thinks, I will have to go.

And who will live with Nitza-the-closet? With the little sun?

His spirit is clear, and he sees the cockroach just as it is. He wants what is present. In the morning—the morning, and so on.

43

He sees how an inner light spreads through his hand. At first through the little finger and then through the other fingers, up to the thumb.

He understands the sacred nature of the hand and the sacred nature of the frying pan, but other things disturb his spirit:

The life line. Breathing (the need for it). Books and generally speaking all things made (like crystal vases). Bible stories (the tablets of the Ten Commandments and so on).

44

The following night he dreams he is dead, but he's cold. He complains that "it's no longer possible to die as one should."

Later he sees (asleep or awake) the creation of the world.

Together with matter, the creator himself is created, and this is the riddle's solution. Everything contains its own cause, like the wave bearing up the foam.

There are no pictures, said that apprehension. No pictures.

45

In the morning he's frightened, as it were, by the sight of the shoe. The dream (he says under his breath) crossed over the boundary of sleep.

He calls Itzik (every number is the last one) and while both are holding on to the cord, he forgets what he wanted to say.

46

It's extremely hard to know just how the cell split.

The philodendron is the axis around which this plot revolves, since it starts everywhere as a kind of enormous mirror, or like windows in a tall apartment building reflecting the movement on the street.

No one's life story can make the philodendron grow to the left or the right.

Yehoahim hangs up the phone. What then?

47

Maybe one should give each step a name.

Or purify oneself entirely at the entrance to churches, like icicles or pigeons in city squares.

Or one should take, like a clerk, a com-
plete inventory: Streetcars. Sun. And so
on.

There's no other month like November.
Everything in its place (apart from death).

48

On the way to the grocery store Yehoahim
stands, like Archimedes, at the edge of
the sidewalk and discovers universal
truths:

Birds cross the sky on diagonal lines.

Human beings lean forward.

Voices come from every direction.

Though things generally descend to earth,
some things (like dust) . . .

(When nobody's looking, he performs a
motion like the foxtrot.)

49

Beneath the neon light he recites the mantra: Bread . . . Cheese . . . Milk . . .

As in a cathedral, women bend at the knee before crates, and everywhere—in cardboard boxes and in cans—lies the body of God.

Light comes from the star to the large window and falls on a long line of laundry detergents.

50

On the way back Yehoahim sees the thrush and the woman who turns in her sleep.

Clouds pass by his chin and move on, and one cannot account for them by the seas' evaporation, but only (he thinks) by dint of tremendous desire.

An endless cord is stretched from the center of Mount Carmel and extends upward, and even the Polish immigrants see it. Two daily papers are spread out below, but the note "La" links distant galaxies, and nothing remains.

BOOK TWO

51

YEHOAHIM HEARS the bus pass by in the street.

For this one requires:

a) ears
b) a bus
c) a world.

b is always changing—sometimes he hears an airplane, and then the plane must be placed in *b*—and *a*, too, sometimes changes (for example, when one *sees* something). But *c* doesn't change because it is the world, which requires itself. It contains a countless number of things, and if we're forced to decide about one of them, it's possible to choose a word that signifies it (the word world, which is also in the world) or a flower.

What *isn't* clear is the sudden turn taken by a fish, or a school of fish, from one direction to another.

52

Now, when he's in the new house, he
hears the cry "Svetlana."

The name hangs for a moment on the
slope of the wadi over the hillside brush,
and the echo (*na . . . na . . .*) reaches,
in all probability, the beach at Atlit.

A short man who calls himself Dr. Neurath speaks to him (he says, "pleased to
meet you") in the stairwell.

53

Inside the empty house he is full of
smoke. Even his heart (a heart that has
already seen distant ships) is burning.

What burns takes on the form of flesh,
and flesh he thinks he thinks flesh what is
flesh.

Wind from the East passes through the
window and through other holes, as
through the hollow bones of a great bird.
All his memories die, like an old Chevro-
let in the afternoon.

54

He sees a dream: Olga has died, but everyone thinks, even though they see her corpse, that she has gone into the next room to polish her nails.

On the stove there's a pot of water that Olga had prepared for herself, in the way that the dead do such things, and a forty-watt bulb (about which everyone is happy) sheds its light on itself alone.

55

In the morning, the sun stands like a huge Rorschach blot in every window.

Yehoahim leaves the bedroom and goes into the bathroom, and from there he goes into the kitchen and outside, at the mailbox, Dr. Neurath is removing a newspaper which, in a short while, will be opened and spread across the table, in the way that boils or syphilis spread across an entire continent.

56

Within his body Yehoahim sees the hyena.

When the door to the house is opened, the hyena, pensive and cautious, goes out into the courtyard.

Yehoahim can fly over the door (he almost flies) but he nevertheless opens the door, and the house is filled with plaster dust, and he looks for his mother and she answers him. She is in the kitchen, but he doesn't know where the kitchen *is*.

Death (he says to himself) death death death death death death death death to . . . d . . . ie. . . .

57

Dr. Neurath (he thinks) is a man well worth befriending. One can get toothbrushes from him and bounce small tennis balls on his window sill.

In the morning he performs a soft-shoe step on his way to the kitchen and the

conversation with him will be conducted
roughly as follows:

—*Death*
—*No!*
—*Death!*
—*No!*

Small trains pass in every direction, and
joy is boundless.

58

In front of the mirror (he thinks) I can
count all the parts of my body.

The head with the holiness that flows
from the sockets of the eyes like a bird of
paradise as all is absorbed in the divine
lens, an entire mountain comes through it.

Hands that are in fact a cloud, and the
chest's slab like a slab of hardened lava,
Lord Lord (he thinks), send me a sign
such as, for instance, a spider.

59

From the beach at Atlit a fog ascends because it is autumn.

All human ties (he thinks) will die now.
The sky will turn into Harlem, with the
chaos and void of rain clouds, and the
smell of water on plaster will bring about a
transformation within the heart.

The face in the mirror, one's own face,
and the wind that comes in the morning
from Atlit were created, he knows, in a
single moment (as one asks, for example,
"now?").

60

I must (he says silently) understand
why—in a world in which there is only a
stack of hay and a foot, *only* these two
things—my wife left me.

Take, for example, (he thinks) the following game: The first one to peep is the
peeper. You spread out in twos and each

person hits the other on the head until the sun comes up and the rooster crows.

Or this one: Everyone lies beneath an imaginary wardrobe and thinks that the sea is coming toward him, but the sea doesn't come, and therefore everyone loses.

In the new house the light bulbs are still exposed, and echoing thoughts bounce from wall to wall, as the children say: *off the wall.*

61

Like a photograph of the Lovers of Zion in Odessa, his heart becomes like a stained glass window and he goes out to the street at ten. The light is extremely diffuse, as though colored pencils had lost their minds.

it is surprisingly easy to go through people. you just aim at their nonexisting center.

It's ten after ten. All the women whose names are Vivien open an umbrella, and some of them open two.

62

The holy words *the rain comes down* come down with the rain over washrooms and butcher-blocks where they slice up the sacred cow and burn it in the furnace they call an oven. *Allahu Akbar!*

What time is it that everyone's going to the bank with their bank books. Obadiah and Ludwig the lawyer, until the doorway is too narrow.

I think (Yehoahim is thinking as a woman now) . . . he loses his train of thought because of the water that the train . . . Suddenly he loves his shoes very much.

(Should someone desire a realistic description of the first rain, here it is: From Odessa they set out by train for Prague and there, on the Charles Bridge, he fell in love with Genya. One should pencil in the swans beneath the bridge because what . . .)

63

At twenty after ten the rain comes up like
a great big fish. The wind gives birth to
other winds. The cypress is like a suitcase
at customs when there's nothing to de-
clare and a multitude of roosters are in
the air perhaps because the ground has
finally grown cold or because of Hitler.

64

Have I already said it's November?

One can see the month at Bank Leumi
where a man (Gluzman) deposits himself
in the lobby, then withdraws and returns
with his mother, and a woman (Ofra
Bachar) opens new accounts.

There's no other bank like Bank
Leumi. Life (like that of little Bo Peep
who lost her sheep) and light are inside
the bank because the ceiling is a celestial
canopy.

65

Mr. Gluzman asks what the account number is and what, with all the plagues and the signs of the end that streams go suddenly red, it's seven something which is so very intimate, maybe six after six, with the foreclosure that stirs the heart, or eight like Auschwitz, which one can't leave.

66

Mr. Gluzman is holding purple fifty-shekel bills, his writings and biography, which one should burn, as did Nahman of Bratslav*, though the scent of the smoke was exceedingly sweet.

    Born (it's possible to read in the smoke). *Geboyren*. Grows like corn, et cetera. Like primordial man, from whose eyes and nose fire issues, he goes to the Alcalay School with his lunch bag and daily sees the sun that was.

---

*A legendary Hasid who instructed his disciples to burn his writings after his death; they did so, and the smoke from the fire was, they said, exceedingly sweet.

67

Attorney Ludwig is sitting in the foreign currency department because he's about to fly to Germany.

Now he has *two* legs, but at the airport in Frankfurt one can't say, because a divine need might arise to greatly increase the number of attorneys' legs just as he's standing with his two suitcases by the sign that spells out *Zoll*.*

One can see him gathering all these legs into the taxi, and one's heart breaks because who will say to him (as once they said), My dear Ludwig, when from his hips a thousand or more descend?

68

What burns (Yehoahim thinks) needs to be burned by the light of the sun, and therefore he goes out to the street and stares like a pagan where it's obscured.

Now, whoever exits the bank (Zweig

Customs (German)

from the grocery store or Shelomoh Ervin,
who lays out solitaire cards on the table)
goes up in flames because the center
of town is on fire as though Van Gogh
had painted the houses and trees. The
source of energy is evident, and the
form of man—symmetrical and broken—
is revealed.

69

It's extremely difficult (Yehoahim thinks)
to understand how the voices pass between the telephone poles. Or between
the stars (he thinks) or between constella-
tions when, for instance, a woman sighs.

More, more, more, for example, when
the world was created in an act of tremendous license. Countless horses emerged
from a single point.

70

Because it's eleven and the sky is so
sexual, he calls Batya.

The words "his mouth" and "her
mouth" are extremely disturbing because

they don't have the sound of a language so much as of an act, like that wringing out that takes place, at the end, in washing machines.

Nevertheless, as in a novel, when it says "he said" or "she said" they speak, but because of Oblivion it's impossible to know just what they speak of. Maybe Time (like history. For example, tomorrow at six).

71

When he steps out of the phone booth he sees other women.

A woman who is entirely white, and it's possible to know from the look of her thighs. An Egyptian woman who walks like a large bird. A woman upside-down, and a woman for whom the glass is broken again and again.

This walking across the earth's crust while the toenails are polished with various colors as though there had never been a tremendous explosion which, to this very day, distances the heavenly bodies with small handbags containing a mirror and rouge, and so on, and what is said like

Listen, or I'm telling you, and all the
while the body is made of light years
(Yehoahim thinks).

(A logical question disturbs his spirit:
Within his shoes is a person barefoot?)

72

At night the shutter creaks in the empty
room.
  Yehoahim passes through his heart into
what is beneath the heart: now he is dead,
and he asks for a glass of water but no one
hears him.
  Deeper still, beneath this death, he is
an infant, and beneath that infant he's an
infant again but he, this infant, has nothing to grasp.
  *Zeig mir, Zeig mir,** someone calls out.
But what is there to show?

* *Show me, show me (German)*

73

Suddenly (at two thirty) he sees that
happiness is located beneath death and
the infant. Like a hanger (he thinks). Like
fox fur. Like a mountain. Like aftershave.
Like trousers. Like walking out through
the front gate of the school. Like the burnt
side of things (toast, for example).

74

In the morning he has a dream: His
father, Ephraim, comes to him, but
the space of the dream is the space of
touching.

He thinks (in the dream): Dreams are
airier. How could the dead be embodied
in flesh?

This thought drives his father (bit by
bit) from the space of the dream, and he's
awakened, because the inner talk about
dreams has driven him toward the Great
Dream.

Here (he thinks) my wife left me, and,
all morning long sea winds come from the
beach at Atlit.

(Pfff! he says to himself just as the world was created.)

75

He looks through the books he brought to the new apartment and finds a novel.

A woman is sitting in the guest room and waiting for a letter, but someone comes in and announces that the hunting dog has been hurt. The woman thinks "this is an evil omen" and looks through her desk for the forbidden letters. In the meantime, the veterinarian arrives and he, too, desires her, and through the French doors she sees that a carriage is approaching and so forth.

76

And what (he thinks) if the carriage is carrying a letter, or the window through which one sees in the book shatters and the sound of glass comes to *these* very ears?

What passes between worlds that *here* there is pain, and there the memory of pain that took on the form of words?

Now his life, too, seems like a story, except that *here* there occur the same eruptions that take place on the surface of the sun, and he hears the sound of this burning, like the song which is of this world *alone*: "Frère Jacques."

77

And what (he thinks) do I want?

A woman. A large woman. A very large woman who will block out every horizon until nothing is left but a single leg in the world.

Take (he thinks), a bookbinder. He binds and binds and binds and binds, and before his death he remembers a cup of tea that he drank.

This (he thinks) is the mystery of the world. A man whose name is Buchbinder, who drinks a cup of tea. Afterward, he sucks on a lemon and adjusts the yarmulke on his head.

(In sorrow he drives the sphere of earth.)

78

In the morning as well it isn't too late to bring back the night, and therefore Yehoahim turns the big map over and brings Dr. Neurath back to bed.

The sound *Svetlana* is also gathered from end to beginning as though in a time tunnel, and the heart, ahh, the heart carries an entire herd of Brahman cattle into sleep.

Now Batya (today at six) enters from below, in the way that people enter dreams, and she is like a beloved for whom a Taj Mahal is built.

Someone from Revlon is distributing an essence of flowers. Woe to the god who's a traveling salesman.

79

Between sleep and sleeplessness he pictures Batya offering him her toes like
Dunkirk when the straits fill up with ships
and the dress (the atmosphere we breathe
in) is crumpled on the floor—a floor that
exists for acts such as this—while the
body (like an iceberg) rises up from the
water and already on its surface there are
white bears and seals and young seals
clinging to their mothers and penguins
who, like short philosophers, march back
and forth in front of invisible desks.

80

On the other side of the wall, against his
will, Dr. Neurath returns to his bed at
seven thirty.

He has psychoanalytic visions: Professor Staub, of Vienna, rests his right leg on
the sill of the window, even though the sill
is higher than his hips. Mrs. Nussbaum is
sitting under a walnut tree, but she isn't
herself, as her face is sinking (her eyes are
reversed and so on) inward.

He, too, hears the shout "Svetlana," but his spirit is heavier because he is German, and where are his toys, his Great Bear, for example. . . .

(Half-dreaming, he's touching the air, like a king.)

81

This second sleep, at seven thirty, while the sun is already shining, draws Dr. Neurath and Yehoahim so close together that they both see a single picture.

A man, with a woman rising from his nostrils (like a genie from a bottle). But now the dream is extremely realistic because the woman is wearing a robe and standing by the sink, but the sink is made of the stuff of dreams, as is the water that issues from its faucet, and, as with alchemy, a base metal is turned into gold and the robe, too, is aglow, and the soles of the feet and the arms, and one could see (if someone stood there) how, beyond the dream, the sheets and the legs of the bed and the

strip of wall by the dreamer's head give
light, too, from within the light within,
and damn him who distinguishes between
these worlds.

82

It is entirely possible that a dream seen by
the light of day is cast in gold if one sees a
landscape (earth and sky). . . . In any
event, Yehoahim gets up on one side of the
wall, and Dr. Neurath on the other, and
both of them look in the mirror.

The faces they see (like when a soufflé
is served up and they say "it's still hot")
are new:

Dr. Neurath performs a step of the
Charleston and, to himself, Yehoahim
sings a Calypso song that Harry Belafonte
sings ("I wonder why nobody don't like
me") as people say, without thinking,
mishmish (and don't say *mishmesh**).

*apricot (Hebrew), the proper, dictionary pronunciation

83

From the village of Kabbabir, a wild cock climbs through the air and sends out a scream over the back of the mountain.

Dr. Neurath moves his face away from the mirror. In the air he draws the sign of infinity, then he walks toward the clothes closet.

Yehoahim opens the window that faces the beach at Atlit. Then he picks up the umbrella and opens it. This (he thinks) is the riddle's solution and, at the same time, he sees that the air is broken.

84

How the air shatters when a man wants.

What can we do with this mystery of names from which nothing can be stripped or derived, such as, for example, a man called (and called) Nikita, who stands before the world.

Mornings in the month of November fill our hearts with memories. We see glass-like butterflies and everything (such as, for example, the words grocery store).

. . . Time's mechanism is more exposed, like machines in the belly of a ship. Happiness, too, sends a crack through the heart.

85

He remembers how once he heard the shopkeeper scream *I don't have any water because I don't have water* and how he understood, for the first time, the principle of cause and effect.

Even facts (he thinks) now stand in the space of the world like a zeppelin.

In his mind's eye he sees how, at six, he enters the Bank Café and Batya is already there, and everyone says what he says until the hands (as in Genesis) go forth on their own.

86

What (he thinks) is all this haggling as though there were no sky. After all, one could extend icons there from end to end.

A kind of primordial man before he was defiled, like an Armenian with light in his nostrils and ears, and whose eyes are deep like clusters of stars. From *there* (from that man) it's possible to go anywhere, even to government ministries.

Now Dr. Neurath is standing again by the mailbox, and he takes out the paper *HaAretz*. There is no end to this holiness, that one can simply take it out as one takes a folded tie in one's hand to look at its pattern: one thing woven into another, and a blaze of color.

87

Nearly nine, and from a crate Yehoahim takes out a coffee grinder he brought back once from Venezuela, though he has never been there, and has never seen a coffee grinder like that, but the word Venezuela . . .

And he also takes out a photo album, where he stood in this place or that and they copied his face onto the paper as they copy a sole in a shoe factory, or a pheasant (which they call *phasianos*) and the pheasant doesn't know to which hill it will fly.

88

Though he's due to meet Batya at six, he has, in the meantime, other visions:

A woman whose name suggests the scent of persimmons is sitting in a taxi and her hand is reaching up to her face. Up to there, she says, but the word *there* isn't heard.

Or a vision like this: Something extremely internal that has no form and only the form of feeling (great pain) shuts it in.

The garbage truck comes down the street, and from the back window one can see two people running after it.

89

All of a sudden, as though for no reason, he picks up a knife and cuts into the flesh of his arm.

Blood comes out of the cut skin and drips toward the sink, since, after all, the sink contains the blood of the world, and it turns with the motion of the earth, and the blood doesn't run the wrong way.

Now the knife is near his neck, but he is afraid of the pain, and that he might shout Shmuel, when his name, after all, is Yehoahim, and his father's name is Ephraim.

90

Yehoahi - m (he silently shouts).

What is it? What is it? What is it? What is it? Did the sandal rip? Did the leather split? Has the water gone salty? The earth been extinguished?

He sees (like an idiot) a million angels whose lips are pursed, and all are playing backgammon.

91

He goes to the closet and takes out the Bank Café shirt. The mirror tells him that he has died meanwhile and one can call him also by another name—Arthur, for instance.

Nevertheless, fields of sorghum are already growing inside the room and birds are fluttering against the window.

how can wheat grow in a room and birds hover over the internal field. the two spaces must be fused since consciousness holds within itself an immense cupboard.

92

My mother (he thinks) was Elizabeth, and now I'm about to meet Batya. The shirt's in place (on the chair), and now he's looking for socks.

He remembers wearily a little girl and this memory (I know! I know! the girl is saying) is folded within another:

A lot of water and sand, but we're going back home. Elizabeth opens the door, and Ephraim hangs the hat on the hat stand. I thought you'd be back at one, says Elizabeth.

93

Later on, when Elizabeth died, Ephraim went at one to the cemetery and the day was delightful. There was a big taxi and someone shouted "Charity saves from death."

The shirt, Ephraim, the Bank Café, and Batya (he thinks) are like the stuff of a great novel someone is writing and the only thing missing is someone (like the foreman he saw once) who will always be shouting "There's no time."

94

Now that he has found a pair of socks, he sees his toes as one sees gold buttons or piano keys.

What are the names of the internal

countries? *That's* where toys are made.
A world-mirror from a fish's diaphragm.
A clock that looks like a blanket.

And what (he thinks) is a woman? A hen.

95

The sun turns over every hour, and now
the clouds are covering it, as in the bus
company's parking lot.

In the house below, Yehoahim sees a
pepper plant on the roof, and people coming and going.

He remembers something about a man
named Lazarus who rose from the dead in
the way that one finds a pickle in a can,
and the shroud (he thinks) had already
darkened with the colors of earth.

This act (he thinks) of my going to the
Bank Café at six, to see Batya, is like that
act, and he puts the white shirt over his
body inside this stadium we call the
world.

96

Silently, he tries out a conversation:

—Hello
—Hello

Or:
—How are you
—Fine, thanks

Or:
—Einstein
—Darwin (or Freud)

Or:
—*Please!*
—*Please!*

97

And what (he thinks) will that place bring
forth when he comes with his white shirt
and Batya sits in her batik dress at the
back of the Bank Café, by Lebanon Gate
Road?

forms will change into the formless and
everything human will turn divine. a huge
bird will hover over the street like an old
battleship.

Because loneliness strikes he lays out solitaire cards on the table, and the numbers
(one to thirteen) close in on him like the
fences of a concentration camp.

98

Four in the afternoon, and the white shirt
is already wrinkled, but the air is filled
with tiny angels known as zephyrs.

The shoreline is going red, and even
though Friday is still far off, the voice of
the muezzin, sick with longing, comes
with the wind from Kabbabir.

These (Yehoahim thinks) are the legs I
will lead to the Bank Café, a grasshopper
like me, alas, and he cries over the sink
into the stainless steel.

Something ascends through this inner
fire and burns toward the ceiling: Life,
which is frighteningly only for once.

99

Like a cow he lifts up a prayer. Like a goat
whose one eye is green and the other a
murky white, or like an albatross, or the
masts of a sailboat, ahh, that once they fed
him and carefully cut up a piece of bread,
as his mouth was still small, and toys (like
a tin duck) surrounded him as though an
old man had arranged his life within hours
that were sweet as sugar cane.

100

The unbelievable: He walks step by step
toward the Bank Café, in infinite space,
across the crust of a star.

BOOK THREE

101

Five to six.

On the other side of the street, Batya walks toward the Bank Café because of the fog and the down quilts people keep in the inner rooms, or their viscera. Though her beauty is external, what nourishes it comes from the dark.

By the supermarket, flesh responds to flesh, as the butcher sees her from behind the glass and the cleaver he's holding dies of love.

102

As in the comics, one could draw a bubble over her head and write in the words "In a little while I'll see him" or "I don't know if" and so on.

She, Batya, has no interest in the sun, and therefore she brings up the moon, which, though grammatically masculine is actually feminine, in accordance with the laws of revelation and concealment.

A little while before the moon goes pale over the insurance office, windows open and shut because Batya is thinking.

103

By the Chinese restaurant Batya's shadow falls on a wall, and she stands there (thinking) as she stood when they told her the baby was Mongolian. Then, too, an entire dimension was taken from her, as though from that day on she was destined to live, as it were, on a piece of paper.

Nevertheless, the shadow holds a kind of life, for the wind lifts up the hem of her dress which is on the wall (the wind's shadow, she thinks) and along the upper thigh (although it's weightless) there appears, in a pallid light, the age-old motion of whoredom.

104

The sauce (she thinks) should be seasoned with capers.

The soles of her feet are sweating inside her shoes, which are autumn shoes, but love's already lying in wait, like a bear, just around the corner.

All this laundry (she thinks) that I hang up day after day, while no one sees me because the roof is high . . . and wasn't I born as though in a war, in which there's conquest and bloodshed—and I myself sought that blood . . .

(A man named Schlief, who remembers her from somewhere, nods his head because what . . .)

105

Let Batya have a marshmallow. Or give her a small bicycle, so she can stand with one leg on it and push herself along.

Violet is her color like the sky in Patagonia, or a field of flowers in the Caucasus

Mountains. The neck that rises in-eluctably from her batik dress shatters our hearts.

See how the moon wavers. Today you can call it Batya, for being's belly is hollow.

106

The gross world (the northern half of the central Carmel*) is the book as it is. The net world consists of the two names, and even less than that.

Give us strength, for it's no longer possible for us to tell the truth at all times (like Allenby Street, et cetera), blind from the host of colors and forms. . . .
   Where is the point at which all roads meet and from which they emerge like lies from a businessman's mouth.

Six o'clock, damn you.

*the mountain range on which the city of Haifa is built

107

Now Batya sees Yehoahim's head by the glass.

She doesn't need glasses, for her eyesight is nearly perfect. But it's hard to fathom why her sight opens out from her and extends.

Someone is calling *Simon*, as though he doesn't believe that Simon will come. And, in fact, two years before the end of the millenium, in November, how could he come?

Time itself has been cast in doubt, and so, space which is cast across it (the head on the street and the head in the pane of glass) comes and goes, like on TV.

108

The mastiff now emerges from Book One and stands again on the other side of the street.

If you'd like music, you can add to these scenes the opening bars of the *St. Matthew Passion*: Someone goes to some-

one, and above them someone unfurls a
sky.

109

It's hard to imagine the crowd at the Bank
Café.

Waitresses come and go, as though the
aisles between the tables were the flight
paths of birds. Clouds of steam rise up
over the espresso machine, and the cus-
tomers move their mouths as in religious
rites photographed for *National Geo-
graphic* in the jungles of the Amazon.

Ludwig the lawyer sits there as well,
with his wife, Paula—they who at night
are naked but whose bodies now are covered with fabric.

110

Suddenly Batya is burning like the bush of
God.

I am the bush (she says to herself) with
the fingernails and the flesh beneath them,
and with hair that flies in the wind and
cannot be held down with pins, and silk

lingerie one can toss toward the ceiling
. . . and from the air they call to me,
milk and water and fire and dust, and
all the photo albums when they said to
me: smile, and something got into me,
through to the innermost walls, holy holy
holy holy, and up she goes to Yehoahim's
place by the glass facing Lebanon Gate
and says, Come.

111

In the hollow within her eyes, the entire
Bank Café is held. The glass brushes up
against the clear matter of the eye like the
moment before the Creation of the
World, when emptiness bordered on
emptiness, and all rang out without a
sound.

Come? Much to our horror, man is,
after all, condemned to distance.

(What would you like to drink? the waitress asks.)

112

Imagine for a moment that a man is
shouting Melville! Melville! in Indonesia.
There isn't anyone there by that name.
But maybe someone whose name is
Sukarno or Suharto will stick his head out
of the doorway and ask: What?

And though it's November, the grapes
have suddenly ripened. Panic has broken
out at the hat store. All sorts of signs bear
witness that things which only seem to be
small, and in fact every gesture, even of
the little finger, can overturn worlds.

113

Now Yehoahim is following Batya step for
step as though he were a camel and the
roofs of the central Carmel were the tops
of mountains at the edge of the desert.
Display windows send back reflections for
an instant and return to their toys' tranquility: large bottles of perfume or rows
upon rows of eyeglasses. Only the moon,

that member, is fat because it's the middle
of the month.

114

In front of the door to the house, Batya
looks at Yehoahim for a moment and
sticks the key into the keyhole.

The key fits (Yehoahim thinks). Like
mountain and valley. Like light and dark.
Like a kiosk and the daily paper. Like a
leg and the hair along it.

She sets the key down on the table in the
hall and in the same motion, from below
to above, strips off her batik dress.

Now Yehoahim can see the buttocks
and spine as though he had turned into
the legs of a horse.

115

He remembers something from the *Bha-*
gavad-Gita. A thousand suns or something of that sort. *Tsinder, Tsinder,* he
thinks. The skin is everything. And the
beauty of the naked and hairy woman

before him sets his heart on fire, so he will
go to her, as one does when heroin goes to
the head or awe comes through the great
churches filled with depictions of lechery.

She undoes the buckle on the belt, and the
pants fall to the floor, thank god.

116

the naked body connects directly to the skies.
as stardust it shines dimly like gold. as flesh
it moves like huge waterplants.

The sound of the tapping on flesh is the
sound of the one hand, for there is no
longer any division between body and
body, ahh, this love for ourselves, like
suddenly turning a light on and seeing.

117

The hands are hands but doubled. The
belly is doubled. The legs are numerous
and the tongue or back of the ear, oh, give
us the other body with utter perfection

as you issued forth from yourself the great
bodies of water before and behind since
the anus is the place where you enter into
this sacred covenant, oh, and once we
played with toys.

118

Now the Mongolian baby is crying and
Batya, naked, goes into the other room.

In the dim light Yehoahim sees a painting by Munch. Not *The Scream*, but the
painter's mother, elongated, severe, a
white wrap on her head.

The sheets as well are strange to him, and
he asks himself all sorts of questions, such
as how Mrs. Munch conceived (naked
and so on) or how, between the heavenly
bodies that rapidly distance themselves
from each other, space, quietly, is filled
with love.

119

Now Batya returns from the other room and the Mongolian baby is between her breasts.

Would you like some coffee, she asks like Vesuvius, from which a flame suddenly flares forth and covers entire cities. So what if he wants some coffee, will the woman and the child boil the water, naked?

He knows that a sight such as this one is seen only once in a thousand years, and therefore he silently screams, like the man Munch painted.

120

Batya sets the Mongolian baby down by Yehoahim and puts on a nightgown. Through the thin fabric, one can see her nipples, like a rainbow appearing after the rain as the sun starts shining and the people point.

Out of the corner of his eye, Yehoahim sees the Mongolian baby's hands and the hands are moving around in the air like dervishes in Konya. He himself (that is to say, Yehoahim) is now thinking, like a Sufi, lewd thoughts about the word "world."

121

World, world, he thinks, and even though another word after this word is called for, once again he thinks only *world, world.*

Batya (*world, world*) brings out the coffee and puts it (*world, world*) by the bed.

This is love, he screams, like the man Munch painted. An entire person stoops over the bed and is called Batya.

122

It's raining outside now and Batya takes in the laundry: A shirt. A towel. Underwear, et cetera. Something about the sight and scent of the laundry reminds him of the

Garden of Eden: Snakes went about on all
fours. The sounds of a flute and a woman
stretching strings, like those of a violin,
between two apples trees, and hanging
transparent dresses from them.

(Do you know Mira? Batya asks, as
though a vase had just fallen.)

123

Suddenly, all at once, the words *Petah
Tikvah** saw through the space of the
room like a cicada in August.

Or also the word *Hoffnung* and *hope*,
because there are also grasshoppers that
make a sound and some of them rub their
hands together like merchants at the dia-
mond exchange.

This, Batya thinks, is love, and her
down quilt is torn clouds.

* *a town near Tel Aviv—literally, The Gateway to Hope*
(Hebrew)

124

The phone rings and maybe it's Robert.
The liar. Who masturbates in the bathtub
like everyone else, and whose hair is
falling out as in the days when farmers
sowed their fields from a sack.

I can't talk now, Batya says, since she's
a sad bird who now is happy, very happy,
on the third floor.

125

The desk lamp casts a triangular light and
now the three of them (Yehoahim, Batya,
and the Mongolian baby) are silent.

Batya lies down on one side of
Yehoahim, and the Mongolian baby on
the other, like pages in an old book that
are almost stuck together and the print is
beginning to blur.

Six hands. Give me (who is not one of
the three), and give the reader, O Lord,
the strength to breathe.

126

The sky is exceedingly clear, and the rain falls straight from the stars.

Each drop finds its place on the ground. This one and this one and this one and this one and again there's no difference between an old wardrobe and a flower.

   It's possible to measure the distance from place to place. Two centimeters here. Thirty there. But what.

127

At 8:00 Batya says: I want to tell you about myself. The Mongolian baby meanwhile has fallen asleep, and she carries him into the other room.

Robert, she says, is courting me, but I don't love him. He just doesn't do it for me. Do you know what I mean?

(A wind comes from outside and ruffles the curtains.)

128

I was with Robert on *Hoshanna Rabba**.
And I was with him on *Hayyechon*.** We
drank from blue mugs and flew to Prague.
But what can I tell you. It was like when
the copies come out of the Xerox machine
with a black stripe down the middle. . . .

A nostalgic music drifts in from elsewhere. Frank Sinatra or Pat Boone. Something in Batya's face has a marble-
like quality and, as a result, or for another
reason, Yehoahim's heart suddenly
flutters.

129

Now he's craving again but this time
in the way one craves a mountain or
smoke.
     He raises his right hand up through the
ceiling and the clouds and grabs hold of

* *A Jewish holiday, the seventh day of the Feast of Tabernacles*
** *Literally, "in the days of your life" (Aramaic), a phrase from
the kaddish, the prayer for the dead*

the moon between his thumb and forefin-
ger. Batya is silent, and only the noise of
the bus reaches them from the street.

(Take one, he says, offering her a round
biscuit.)

130

The baby isn't Robert's, she says. But I
don't want to discuss it. Would you like
some more coffee?

She goes barefoot to the window and
her toes refute the theory of relativity.
There aren't (Yehoahim thinks), in the entire world there aren't any other toes like
these, and he swears to himself that he'll
trim her toenails with tremendous care,
toe by toe, and be especially careful when
he comes to the place where the nail enters
the flesh as one is careful in reading a
philosophical argument so as to be sure it
all adds up.

131

"Hey," says Batya (where she should have said "Listen," and therefore his heart goes out to her) . . . "Hey," she says, and Yehoahim almost shouts "I hear you," as the children of Israel shouted at the foot of the mountain and took it upon themselves to observe the entire Torah, and he, too, wants to observe the commandments (for example, the commandment regarding good morning when rising to brush one's teeth after she comes out of the bathroom) like an extremely religious person who follows the scent of the toast and coffee into the kitchen that they call Mecca.

132

Things happen, like the water dripping from the broken faucet. Gestures. A gust of air. Thoughts. A bird or the shadow of a bird. Books, and Heaven help us.

Yehoahim utters his name (silently) in order not to lose it, and Batya does something internal that cannot be disclosed.

133

How, they're thinking like a Greek chorus, how can we bring this love into the world? Sometimes, after all, one drags one's feet and looks for aspirin or an eye is swollen (they think together) or the soul wants to be elsewhere. . . .

It's already 9:00, and, as on one's birthday when an extra candle is lit for the coming year, they clasp hands, their fingers meshing (ten altogether), and each finger meets in the other's hand another one like it, like two women sitting at a café and reminiscing about Bucharest.

134

Stay a little longer, Batya says.

Munch's mother is on the wall, beneath her a glass fawn that someone blew in Venice. The palm being held is warmer than the other, like the lit side of the earth, and time is being formed (despite what Einstein thought) from rest.

The two of them recall other loves, and the heart, thank god, beats with the other's, like going together to a museum and stopping, now here, now there.

135

My wife left me, Yehoahim says.

He sees the empty house and Nitza-the-closet but now the pain has grown dull, as though it were coming from the other side of the wall.

Batya runs the fingers of her free hand over Yehoahim's chin, and makes the sound of a B-flat.

(Imagine, for a moment, the death of God. That great body ceases to breathe and nevertheless we're all within it.)

136

At 9:30 the Mongolian baby is crying again but Batya doesn't get out of bed.

The baby is crying the pain, as it were, of the world, not his own individual pain.

Crying the motion of those cement mixers that stand on lots where new homes are being built. Crying the price tags the grocer places at the edge of a crate. Crying all these, in a low cry like a dirge, and Yehoahim requires extraordinary strength not to die.

137

Two (he says to himself) two, two . . . what good is it all and we're still two?

He goes back to the place where it all began, before he was born and before the birth of the world. Before there were even the silhouettes of mountains, and how is it possible to cut through something that's empty?

What brought about (he thinks) all this multiplicity, so that in the end a man walks along, his name (Rosenberg) clinging to him as though there were no world at all?

138

Suddenly (what do you mean, suddenly?
at a quarter to ten) Batya says I love you,
and a tremendous happiness fills his heart.

Now he understands the great mystery:
everything is split in appearance only, and
he can contain even Munch's mother.

139

Also (he thinks) inside the eye. And also
inside the liver. And on newsprint. In gra-
nola and yogurt too. And in gardens. And
beyond gardens, in lightning and flashes
during the night. And in endless darkness
when one exits the galaxy and not even
the sight of a star exists and one remembers only a single toy (a doggie doll, or a
cat).

140

Take a word (Yehoahim says to himself).
Take a word like son, thy son, thine only

son, in that scene where Abraham drew the knife, like "yes," or like "let there be," or like "Jehovah," just so long as you don't make a mistake, for if you make a mistake creation will take everything back, as when one regrets a momentous act and reverts to no-thing. I can't afford to make a mistake, he thinks to himself, and, therefore, his lips mouth the only word that holds all of these worlds: Batya.

141

Batya removes the earring from her right ear. The silver gives me an infection, she says. The desk lamp shines on the roots of her hair, and Yehoahim sees that some are white.

Ever since I saw you, she says, last year, I've hoped that you would call me.

What a peculiar word, Yehoahim thinks, hoped, hoped. I hoped too, he says, but doesn't know what.

142

All my life, Batya says, I've looked for someone who would understand this. Now she takes off the other earring, and Yehoahim sees the hole in the lobe.

Things are distant, he thinks, truly distant. Like lights you see from within a train and you know that people are eating dinner out there, but *you* will never know this.

143

The Mongolian baby is speaking to himself now, words like bayoo or bah-oo.

Batya turns on the radio and the news comes on: The laundry in such and such a place has dried faster than expected. A certain apple is full of worms. Dust covers the kitchen utensils and someone is crossing the street.

Where she is, on the other side of the world (Yehoahim thinks), the sun certainly rolls over twice, and he touches Batya's back, like a breeze grazing the ground.

144

This, then, is happiness, he thinks. And as a result his heart breaks in folds like a mountain when the lava rises. Like the splinters of chairs on a café patio after a bomb has gone off, now half of him is dead and the other half is looking at death. He realizes that he has to go, but his feet are very cold, like Socrates' when the poison had gone halfway through him.

I'm going out on the balcony, Batya says, and he sees her go out to a place where there isn't any balcony, and there she stands, three stories up in the air over the sidewalk.

145

Yehoahim puts on the clothes he'd draped over the chair, shirt and pants, and Munch's mother stares at him from the wall.

On the counter he sees a letter, and since the paper is crumpled up he reads only "I also saw the Grand Canyon and believe me . . ." (and he sees a woman standing at the edge of the huge canyon).

Suddenly he is thirsty, but Batya's on the balcony and it's dark in the kitchen and the spirit of God is hovering over the face of the waters.

146

At ten-thirty Yehoahim drinks lemonade and Batya wraps—in white paper—a tomato and a cucumber that he needs for breakfast.

All theories (he thinks to himself) of creation can be refuted, for space itself was created from a kitchen table, and time—from the motion of two hands.

Do you want some olives? she asks, and something in his soul cries out: Yes! Yes! Yes! Yes!

147

Now, as in a novel being written by a woman writer from Finland who was stricken with polio, Yehoahim stands at the door, holding a paper bag in one hand and an umbrella in the other.

Of all possible questions, Batya chooses to ask: "Will I see you tomorrow?"

You'll see . . . Yehoahim thinks. Rays of light will strike me, break, and progress in a straight and broken line toward the two lenses you're carrying inside your eyes. The image of light will rise like an electric current toward your head and *there* you'll see me, deep within.

148

In the stairwell Yehoahim notices graffiti. Someone has written "God is hairy," and through the latticework on the first floor he sees a strip of sky full of stars.

The stars . . . he thinks, but his thoughts reverse themselves, in the way one turns a coat inside out, and now it's the stars that are thinking.

Man (they think) is only a kind of chop meat, and, nevertheless, at times he says things like: "Where are you, Eurydice?"

149

The street is beyond description as the heart has begun to overflow its banks like cats coming out of a trash bin. Houses and the houses of houses lean aside, and smoke rises up to the sky. A large thrush shrieks The Messiah is Coming and the moon, feminine and full, hangs there as though in a painting.

Love, like a silkworm, also spits up December.

150

Take him, lead him by yourselves to his bed on Margoliot Street.

Let someone ask him, on the corner of

Kabbabir, what time it is. Let him take off his shoes and set them beside one another, like the shoes that Van Gogh painted. Count his limbs, two by two, and so forth, and don't forget to tuck him in with the down quilt because of his heart, on account of his heart which is under the quilt.

BOOK FOUR

151

BATYA IS sleeping in the way one descends from the apex of a right triangle straight down to the base of the vertical leg.

Her dreams wax full (with milk, et cetera). And even in her sleep she knows that a miracle has taken place (like a wind blowing the fishing boats back to shore).

Apart from that, the night is full of the chirpings of bright-colored birds called by ancient names and the screaming (as though of a trombone, or contrabass) of very large fowl.

152

All sorts of words come to her, with an explanation beside them:

a mule— a bird, half-horse and half-cow

a door— a wide path that opens and
closes

gloves—   hands

blueberries—   pumpkins on which one
                can climb to the sky

She turns over in her sleep toward the wall
and there in that chill, for a moment, she
finds death.

153

Robert rings the doorbell in the morning,
and when Batya opens the door he asks:
Who was here yesterday?

Now it's already December and the
earth's axis points to the north, and likewise Robert changes with the season. He
drinks coffee in the kitchen (his arms,
both of them, in the air), and the sun
climbs in the windowframe in the way
that one takes a box of tobacco out of an
inner pocket.

154

Yehoahim rises like a foot at half past seven, wraps his body in a bathrobe, and sits down to write:

Dear Berman,
In your last letter you argued that Quantum Theory involves an inconceivable logic according to which a thing is both itself and not itself. Last night I understood that such a logic is in fact quite feasible.

How is the horse you take out of the drawer each morning?

Through the window he sees birds. Seven or eight.

155

Since the bathroom faces East, he sees the sun through it.

Good morning (he thinks), dear sun. Are you, too, in love? Perhaps with the moon, which is always fleeing and leaving you a pale reflection? Call her back and tell her, Come to me with your children the stars. Primordial man (which is to say, me) will put his two hands together and the heavenly bodies will return to their original positions.

156

He tears up the letter he wrote to Berman and writes another:

My Dear Berman,
I hope you're recovering from your flu. Here the sun is still shining, and even though it's already December, there hasn't been enough rain. I miss our conversations about Quantum Theory and other things, for, as you know, it's hard to find a friend like you.

He takes an umbrella out of the closet, and, by God . . . at the iron tip, a white light glimmers as though the sparks coming off of lower matter were revealing themselves to the eye. The eye itself can contain an infinite number of umbrellas instead of his wife who had only a single body and now she's at Ramot HaShavim.*

157

Now Robert rises from the table, and because he is wearing a shirt, he carries (like Moses) the Ten Commandments.

Thou shalt not, in particular, commit adultery, and even though he himself has committed adultery he issues an order to Batya like curdled milk, or milk in which one places a wick and fire rises from that wick and the milk melts, and you determine the time: *until* then—pre-history. From then on—two to the start of the candle and so forth.

I am a woman she screams (feminine fire) and you cannot make my life into something like buying a ticket for a movie at the theater downtown. What do you know—walking around like a saw-in-pants.

* *a small town near Tel Aviv, literally, The Heights of Those Who Return (Hebrew)*

158

Now the sun is aligned with the window,
like a kitsch painting, thank god it's there,
and not somewhere else, like the vegetable
stands on the road to the north, where
everything is set out in its place and you
can also find an old refrigerator whose
utter randomness appeals to you: note,
dear reader, how I'm undressing Batya,
and we'll have her on the floor like dying.

159

The Mongolian baby is crying now, wail-
ing, because morning for him is a kind of
beginning, and he hears the voices from
the kitchen and remembers that he stood
at Mount Sinai and even there he heard:
Go, Go, Go out beneath the skies, for
everything happens outside and within,
such as, for example, the door being
slammed, and also the doors that are
valves of a heart through which blood
flows, and the heart itself misses a beat as
when flying over Nagasaki, an atom bomb
in the belly of the plane, for we are, after

all (Batya and everyone), human beings, and who will love us?

160

At 8:00 Yehoahim again hears the scream "Svetlana." Something goes off to Atlit and returns like a very slow boomerang.

He opens the umbrella in order to check it, but in fact he would like to fly away like Mary Poppins over the homes of people in his long johns and shirt which says: BE HAPPY.

This heart (he thinks) which is always beating, beats on its own. And how could he come to the heart of another? He suddenly sees the miracle itself, like the conjugation *ahavti ahavta ahavnu,** where the root holds fast and the suffixes draw it outward, Blessed art Thou, O Lord, our God who is good for nothing.

*I loved, you loved, we loved

161

He raises a plate and says blue blue blue blue blue blue blue blue blue blue blue blue blue blue blue blue blue blue blue blue blue blue blue blue blue blue blue blue blue blue blue blue blue blue blue blue blue blue blue blue blue blue

162

Till 9:00. At 9:00 he turns off the water and puts the transparent plate in the place where the dishes belong, as Zeus took hold of the planet Venus and, for a moment, brought it down and showed it to the Athenians so they would open the city gates for him and he could enter, tired, and get into bed.

163

After Robert leaves, Batya remembers her name. If I am Batya, she thinks, who is Batya really?

The whirlpool that comes from the wall engulfs her like crepe-paper ribbons, and all around her the crowd, as though seated in an amphitheater, cheers her on: Hurrah, hurrah!

She touches the phone but not yet, she thinks, and, meanwhile, the five fingers of her right hand move into place.

164

Her sacred legs are spread by the sacred sink at the precise hour when divinity brings about face-to-face coupling and face-to-back coupling because she is longing for herself, even though her body is light, but the powers of increase within her are drawn down toward those of the toes, each of which is called Batya as well, and they are wet with a pleasure that floods the world.

165

Now she breaks a plate as Moses broke the stone Tablets of the Law, and the shards glitter on the kitchen floor, because the kitchen has a floor, and the floor has a floor, and so on, *ad infinitum*.

The Mongolian baby is laughing now because he's getting to know his very own hands: the wonder of the ten fingers.

166

In the meantime, we have forgotten Dr. Neurath. On account of the tranquility that has descended on Yehoahim, he (that is, Dr. Neurath) is flying.

It's true that Dr. Neurath is flying like a rat (when rats fly) but in his right hand he's holding a copy of Husserl's *On Coughing and Prayer*.

Pieces of toast float in the air of the kitchen because they spring up out of the toaster with a power greater than that of the spring, and in the empty room—amazing—a hoopoe is singing.

167

Yehoahim loves himself in the way that a coffin loves the wood it's made from, or as space loves the planets and stars.

His right hand moves for the phone, but he brings it back because he has got to get into an inner bus whose color is blue, he and his heart, which is full of alleys like Katmandu.

168

His hand moves again toward the phone and he dials Batya's number. But when he hears the sound on the other end he hangs up for now he has to travel on that bus of his all alone, or along with the ghosts of his life, and each of them sees what it sees through a different window and what (he thinks) are these windows if not the windows of the death toward which each of us moves and where is love.

169

What actually happened? Batya asks herself. She's hanging the laundry out to dry
on the balcony and humming a prayer.
Munch's mother is now being struck from
the right by light, and the wrap on her
head is whiter.

The feet's happiness, Batya thinks, is the
happiness of each individual foot, and the
hands' happiness—is the happiness of
each single hand, and she sticks the
clothespins onto the line like a composer.

170

The water is boiling and the steam
rises out of the spout of the kettle, thank
god.
   She invites herself to tea that is made
from fruit, and now her hand is on the
phone, that Sweet Singer of Israel, and she
dials one, as in the Creation, before two
had come into existence, and eight as in
infinity, and six like a goat in the field, and
who knows what goes through the goat's

mind when he leaps, and four on account
of the air, for if it weren't for the air . . .
and twice nine for there *is* no ten unless
you cut yourself and draw blood.

171

Now on the other end of the line a voice
answers as in the Torah when the words
"Where art thou" are spoken.

 The image of the body is absent, but
the voice wandering alone like Orpheus in
the depths of the earth comes to her and
calls her name, which is no longer Batya
but something far more internal, like the
names of volcanoes when the lava pours
forth from them, like the first light de-
stroying the words that brought about its
creation.

172

His name, which he hears (she says
Yohim) breaks the inner windows. It
brings back the night, and again nothing
separates him from himself, except that he
wants to die on account of the sweetness,

like one sound dying into another, like
hearing her say I love you.

*now these are the two heavenly bodies. both
holding a telephone as though somebody
much greater holds his breath for them in
the midst of ten thousand flowers.*

173

What can be said, dear reader, about this
conversation? Give me something with
which I might write the heart out for you.
Your heart, for example, with its mantle of
blood. What do I want?

See how the sun grows feet and moves like
a spider. Where have you brought us,
enormous mass of fire? A person, and another person, and a phone—and what will
we do?

174

Meanwhile, we've forgotten the world.
For instance: Who is Svetlana? Ludwig
the lawyer and his wife. Variatzia the

waitress whose heels click against the floor. Itzik who has business to do, and others (like Robert, who is inhaling now, and exhaling).

(And what of the butterflies, which one sometimes sees in December as well, or Pritzker's new building on Panorama Street?)

175

All the things that we do not see overtake us from behind. Graves, for example. And we haven't yet talked of the air, or the lightair, when they're together like strawberries. So that we can see the Swatch watches with their various colors or the antennae over the billboards, as in ancient Assyria noblemen had wooden dentures carved for them so they could laugh unabashedly.

176

Each of them (Batya individually, and Yehoahim individually) is taking steps at home, but together they're dancing a tango. The dance hall is the universe, with the great lamps hung on high, and the music is the sound of the steps themselves.

Batya goes to the health clinic and walks up to Pirhiya the nurse, for a rash has broken out on the baby's body, and on the way there she also sees, although it's December, all sorts of weeds breaking into flower.

177

Pirhiya the nurse is also within the universe, and she fiddles with her fingers, for what else would she do with her fingers. From every direction her name is being called, Pirhiya, and this is because people know, and they're sure she exists even behind the locked door. A certain Mordechai is especially sure that the outside world also exists beyond thought.

178

In general. Because it's December, and the end of the year, all sorts of women wearing glasses are going out and coming in.

There's no other place like the Histadrut health clinic, where one can count the legs of all the people and divide the total in half. People ask one another what number do you have, like in the Garden of Eden before what happened happened.

179

Today Yehoahim is having an extremely profound conversation with Dr. Neurath about the Tenants' Committee.

About the stairwell, and how the man who washes the floor gets up to the roof but the door is locked and in fact they need to put a layer of tar between the concrete and the sky, because water comes down through the stone into the rooms on the top floor, oy, and the years, as though they were time, but it's impossible to spread them out under the sky, and if we could (Yehoahim thinks) we'd fall on each other's necks and Dr. Neurath would say, Call me Kurt.

180

Now it's balloon season. Take a greenish-yellow balloon and see how it rises. Or one that's dark red, like congealed blood, or white with the color of whitewash or green like spinach, and see how they rise, the colors of the sky adding a soft blue to them, as though the soul had asked about something and answered itself, and asked again and answered yes.

181

We'll go to the greengrocer (Yehoahim thinks), Aberjil, and he will tell me what it costs.

And Aberjil will say the tomatoes are such and such, because, you see . . . the tomatoes are here. And the cucumbers are such and such. And the peppers. Take some kiwi. Batya loves you, I know (Aberjil says). Take care of that love

like I—as you see—take care of the
vegetables.

182

On the way back home from the clinic
Batya sees the trees' shadows which, in
December, are naked as the trees themselves, and her own shadow and the
shadow of the baby carriage pass through
the treetops.

An inner voice tells her Cry, Cry, and
therefore tears stream down her cheeks,
like what one sometimes sees on the walls
of apartments when the plaster begins to
crumble.

There is no end to it (she thinks), and
nevertheless here I am walking around
under the sun.

183

At the corner of Moriah Street she meets
Pirhiya the nurse from the clinic. One can
see that Pirhiya the nurse is busy because
she goes into the grocery store and asks

them to make her a sandwich with yellow cheese.

For no reason at all, Batya recalls the words "the streets of the river," and, when she sees Pirhiya's thin arms, she looks off in another direction.

184

She puts her things (two yogurts, et cetera) onto the baby's lap and pushes the carriage forward to the place where space and time come together. The world's ceiling is made of a bluish marble.

On the Bauhaus-style balcony women are airing out rugs and the clap of the fabric against the stones sounds like a twenty-one gun salute.

Almost out of desperation (she thinks) I'm going toward love.

185

During the afternoon Yehoahim dreams the words *the mountain is falling on me I am drunk.*

186

He sees a fly on the window pane.

I could (he thinks) die now, but I am alive.

187

A cry of alarm comes from the direction of Atlit, but the bird he sees doesn't move.

All sorts of images are turned upside down in his head: this one and this one and this one but the sum-total-of-it-all is transparent like light, and he sees through it even though there's nothing to see.

Nevertheless, the world is full of colors, and even the frame which is grayish-yellow is whole, like the spectrum, with a thousand reflections.

188

Sometimes, at this time of day, a daughter of the sea appears carrying memories like smoke from chimneys when the large factories sound their *toot— toot*—and everyone walks off for a lunch break.

All is given (Yehoahim thinks) and almost all is taken away, and he longs again for Batya's face like a lake that wants the reflections things leave on it.

189

Now Dr. Neurath rings the doorbell and he brings him a receipt for payments made to the Tenants' Committee.

Kurt too (Yehoahim thinks) lives in the world, and he too has an angel of his own that lowers his eyelids night after night, and therefore he asks him in and sits him down beside the window with a view to Atlit.

190

I had a wife (says Kurt) and she died.

191

In the afternoon, Munch's mother enters the shade as the sun sinks in the west.

The Mongolian baby is sleeping, and a thin bubble opens out from his mouth, and so long as he's breathing the bubble trembles.

This is three o'clock, which is beyond the parts of the body that come in twos (eyes, et cetera), but the heart which is one is full, at three, of love.

192

The reader can see all sorts of things at three. Glass cups, for example.

Perhaps he can see how, from an ovule the size of a pea, a person is formed, and that person thinks thoughts such as, for instance: the horizon is full of birds.

193

The reader can also see how the large hand of the clock points to one and later to two and then to three, for what is a novel if not this passage of time.

And space: like the towels that Batya hangs out to dry, like the plea one lifts up before the Holy One, blessed be He, who responds.

194

After Kurt leaves, Yehoahim fills the bathtub with warm water and lowers his body into it.

We haven't yet spoken of Yehoahim's body. He has, wonder of wonders, a form in which hand is like hand and eye like eye, et cetera. The light strikes him like a stick of phosphor and breaks. His scrotum is ancient, like those bindings of the Babylonian Talmud, and within the movement of his legs one sees the wind.

195

Now he is in the bathtub, and he divides the lower waters from the upper waters.

The steam rises and covers the windows, because elsewhere a man named Krochmelnik has died, and they cover the great mirrors there with black cloth, so no one will see the reflections that people impress on them.

At the dead man's home the widow remembers, and so Yehoahim wraps his body in a large towel and moves toward the clothes closet.

196

There are words (Yehoahim thinks), like *tsorn,* whose end we will never know.

Now the room is glowing like a cathedral because the sun is sinking toward the sea, and the shirts in the closet are, as it were, lined up to eat the flesh of God and drink his blood.

From the empty room he hears other sounds, but who knows what that word is.

197

Four.

The Mongolian baby wakes up and sees the marvels of the ceiling. He joins line to line until he has built the Taj Mahal and one can see the palace's double there in his eyes.

198

Batya opens a book containing the innermost streets of Katmandu. And she, too, sees how her life has been doubled as though in a shattered mirror.

I need to go to the cardiologist, she thinks, though her heart is whole and pumps blood through its arteries and chambers. Boom-boom. Boom-boom. Boom-boom. Boom-boom.

199

Amidst all these things, a bird, as well, enters the room, and it's possible to call it a bird.

Its colors are endless, because they shift with the passage of time, like those huge wheels on the ships that traveled the Mississippi a century ago.

Put on a record. Paul Robeson singing "Ol' Man River," and see how you go to the right place.

200

Today (she thinks) I'm going to meet Yohim, and the baby will come with me.

BOOK FIVE

201

(SOMETIMES THE heavens close, and then the Madonna and child cannot descend).

At five Batya falls asleep.
Her sleep is troubled, and in it she talks (saying), "I am Batya. *Bat* (the daughter) *ya* (of God)."

202

A breeze wafts in from the window, but it's impossible to know if the window is in the outside world or a dream.
Now childhood is beginning all over again: Countless feet in the mud. Hair ribbons. Suns as though they were tied by a string to the moon. A large doll. The colors of Thankgod, and the Sambatyon of stars.

203

The word "because" comes to her in its childish form (because because because

. . .). The forehead touches the bathroom sink and all is more.

(The dream is half-truth, half-lie, but even the lie is true in the way that one hears the water in the drainpipe.)

204

Afterward the happiness spreads.

She acknowledges the day-to-day in a single act: attaching socks to the line, or rinsing the spoon.

Light and dark are all mixed up. The light recalling the darkness and the darkness the light like seeing, in winter, the plum tree flower.

205

It is now the time when Batya should be at the Bank Café and she's sleeping. She sees how the Japanese are bombing Pearl Harbor.

The sun is already setting into the sea (or the globe is turning away from it), and from the way that the shadows have lengthened one can see it is late.

On MTV, Madonna is singing silently about how she conceived and gave birth to a child. At 6 o'clock he has six wings and the appearance like the appearance of God.

206

Everything is now confused, as it is in a book where someone has torn out the pages and one has to skip from 72 to 96. A sentence breaks off, unfamiliar characters surround the protagonist—and what happened on the missing pages?

(Maybe a perfect love. Everyone stopped, as though at the sound of the siren on Holocaust Remembrance Day.)

207

We need to take Yehoahim out of this book. So he'll go to Batya at six-thirty and ask, Why didn't you come to the Bank Café.

So he'll take hold of her by the door (*beyond* the book) and press her body against
his, in the way that small parts are sol-
dered to iron wires, in factories where
transistors are made.

208

Yehoahim sits at the westernmost edge of
the Bank Café, and at the northern edge
sits Ludwig the lawyer, like a Protestant,
and beside him sits his wife.

The empty space is very painful, and
Yehoahim thinks of death in the way that
one suddenly thinks of street cats.

209

At six-thirty he calls Batya.

As though in a novel "he hears her
drowsy voice," and suddenly the central
Carmel is glowing as though on a summer
night at the North Pole. The ladders at the
hardware store extend themselves, and at
that moment the shoe-store display window turns into a dance floor.

210

I fell asleep, Batya says beneath the stars.

Imagine that nothing existed. Not even time. Who would have pictured a tree?

(Now Yehoahim is walking toward Batya's apartment because the world was created.)

211

By the door he thinks about the words *by the door,* and the two o's of the word *door* seem to him like testicles.

Likewise a thought about King Saul flickers through his head. His melancholy. The harp. The strings.

212

There's a thirty-watt bulb above her door and maybe therefore Yehoahim does not ring the bell.

The stairwell is a world unto itself, and one could dance a tango there.

213

Now, in the stairwell, the thirty-million-watt sun is shining, as after the words "Let there be" were uttered. The world still withdrawn into a single point without dimension.

The light and the door (Yehoahim thinks). *The light and the door.*

214

Behind the door Batya is putting on a blue robe like a prehistoric mammal.

Love comes between them like a magnetic field and warps the stairs as though their reflection had passed through a crystal ball.

In general. Love is a kind of giant Chagall that lifts cows off the ground and causes tremendous clocks to fly.

(What time is it now, Batya says, as though on a page of a great novel, upper left.)

215

Batya's bare feet contain the Old Testament, which is extremely erotic, what with Bathsheba on the roof and Lot's daughters.

Strange, Yehoahim thinks, that there's also a circle in the word *open*. One can enter the word and arrive at the thing itself.

Within this thought he spreads his arms wide, and Batya comes to the walls of his heart as a cloud enters a mountain.

216

Maybe I'm ill, Batya says, and Yehoahim feels that her body is warm and there's no longer any doubt about it.

Now everything reverts to stardust, as in the painting by Vincent van Gogh, and behind her back he sees a strip of kitchen and a bowl with a cucumber in it.

217

Batya breathes and Yehoahim breathes, Batya breathes again, and Yehoahim too, and again Batya breathes and Yehoahim takes a breath as well. And another breath. Like in a clock store, where all of the clocks point more or less to ten-forty, and one hears the ticking from every direction.

218

Zold mautau bach, Yehoahim says.

Bau, my dear, Batya says.

Now they are speaking as though in a novel and we know what lies beyond the visible.

The facts of her life, for example: *salim* and *argol* within all those *perakhot* and so forth. Or her suffering on account of the trout or things that descend.

(A man named Shimkin walks out of another door and goes down the stairs.)

219

Now Batya is lying in bed, and Yehoahim steeps tea for the first time.

The love between them is exceedingly clear in the space of the kitchen and continues to evolve like a cathedral by Gaudi.

(Was there, in the past, Yehoahim thinks, a man whose name was Me'ir?)

220

Batya's temperature is 101° and, because of the tea, beads of sweat appear on her forehead.

Hallelujah! Thank you for all the mercies, like skin, for instance, which envelops us, or fingernails, and the shadow a kettle casts on the table, and the lamp within which a filament burns like, in the Bible, that bush.

221

Love, Yehoahim thinks, is like a state visit. You bring the guest to all the most beautiful places.

He seems to think that he hears the Kabbabir muezzin. But in fact he is hearing another muezzin, something like an ancient uncle.

Numerals fly like flocks of pigeons, as though the elements were showing themselves with nothing held back.

Death stands in the air, quite naturally, in the way one takes one's place at the table for lunch. Life is playing backgammon with him.

222

If Robert comes, Batya says, don't let him in.

Suddenly Yehoahim understands the words *my life*, and a great terror comes over him.

223

Batya shuts her eyes and sees lines of light.

She remembers an old story about a pair of pants. Someone sewed them, or something like that, and in the end they were useless.

Or they were useful because they were sewn, that is, all the pieces of fabric were joined so the wind would come through them as though through a tunnel.

(See how time passes, and time's nephew—space—is yawning)

224

I feel like going to a Greek island, Batya says. From time to time, the Mongolian baby smiles like the small islands in the Danube, on the way out of Budapest.

From the far side of the wall Yehoahim hears a knocking, as though someone there were trying to flee.

Me too, he says.

225

Suddenly Yehoahim hears his own breathing. A loud noise like a flash flood in the desert, or wind through the ravines.

When the quiet returns, he realizes that someone else is breathing inside him, maybe a man whose name is the same as his.

He looks out the window and sees two moons. The moon one always sees, and another.

226

We'll go to a Greek island, Yehoahim says, but he doesn't have six hundred dollars. He has an old jewelry box and a fan.

He sees Batya's red face on the pillow, Munch's mother, and the Mongolian baby, and asks himself: what am I doing here?

227

Before everything (he thinks) *what*. The great *what* through which colors are strewn from the dawn of time, and he is like Leviathan. Then (he thinks) *I*. As though the word contained no abyss, and one could see it at all sorts of shows. . . .

In her bookcase he sees three volumes of the *Jewish Encyclopedia*: the Aach–Apocalyptic Lit. volume, the Italy–Leon volume, and the Leon–Moravia volume, and therefore (he knows) the love he holds for her is limitless, like the nests of termites (or white ants).

228

My love for Batya (he thinks) is also my love for the Mongolian baby, and my love for Munch's mother, and my love for this sink. And the air's roots in those rooms, in the way one sometimes asks what time it is and the man on the street says it doesn't matter. *All* times are yours.

During the winter flights are cheap, says Batya. That is, one grabs hold of the wing of the plane, as in a picture by Chagall.

229

Night falls like the words Pontius Pilate. The aspirin is taking effect, and Batya's face is paler.

The number of my digits (Yehoahim thinks) and hers together comes to forty, and he is filled with wonder. Earth revolves in vast space, like a soccer ball at the penalty kick.

230

Come, Batya says, lie down beside me.

It's hard to describe the simplicity of this act. How the pants and so on, like the movement of a cloud or a ripple (on the surface of the water).

This warm body (Yehoahim thinks) is called Batya, and he hugs it as an Orthodox Jew hugs the scroll of the Law.

231

All sorts of things stir in the dark. The spirits of the dead for instance.

Aunt Christina, who died when the Italians bombed Tel Aviv, and someone who died of heartbreak.

The dead are transparent, but Yehoahim can hear the sound of their motion in the air, like the celestial music made by the stars.

Aunt Christina fills the space between the dresser and the bed. Her hair is tied up in a bun, but her feet are bare like Beethoven's when he wrote the Ninth Symphony.

232

The white sheet that covers Batya and Yehoahim resembles a shroud, May His Name be Exalted and Sanctified. Love (Yehoahim thinks) is a kind of burial society that comes and purifies your corpse, like worms or the waters of the deep.

He suddenly sees a thousand ships anchored offshore, the large iron links of the anchors' chains emerging from a round opening in the bow.

233

Love me, Batya says, and as on *Simhat Torah** Yehoahim is filled with devotion and presses her body against his own in an ancient act and she cries out, and the Mongolian baby wails, and Robert knocks on the door, and all the voices are heard, as during the hour when the Torah was given as the sun rose over the mountain and the assembled hordes bowed to the ground.

234

Suddenly Yehoahim understands the Muslim call to prayer in the name of God.
Flesh comes into flesh, Allah. Flesh. Allah. Allah. Allah. Like earth and rain,

* Literally, *The Rejoicing of the Law* (Hebrew): *the holiday celebrating the end of the annual cycle of Torah readings, when the Torah scrolls are paraded around the synagogue.*

when the water fills all of the cracks in the ground and the earth breathes.

(Don't let Robert in, Batya says, and Yehoahim almost faints.)

235

Batya open up, Robert shouts from the other side of the door, but Batya hugs the Mongolian baby until he falls silent.

Now the mouth of Munch's mother is open wide, and she is screaming the scream on the bridge. The surface of the picture is the surface of the world, and the scream breaks the frame and enters other dimensions.

236

Maybe Robert is screaming. Maybe the voyagers in space who burned up in that explosion. Maybe prehistoric animals that

were covered by ice. Maybe Walt Whit-
man. Maybe Pirhiya from the health
clinic, whose arms are so very thin,
and maybe it's me, Yoel Hoffmann,
screaming.

237

It's hard to believe, but suddenly the sun
is shining. At half past 9 o'clock in the
evening it's shining on the ceiling, as
though the room were the world, and its
two ends were two horizons.

Within the room all is created anew: the
twin bed. The dresser, et cetera, like enormous icebergs rising up out of the water.
 Names, too, are created, and the baby's
name is Jonathan, and Yehoahim receives
his name, and Batya hers, in the way a
general pins a medal to the chest of an
outstanding soldier. The caption "this is a
family" flashes across the ceiling, as
though being drawn by a small airplane.
Everything has its name, and the name
has one as well.